ACTION MAN

MISSILE ALERT

First published in Great Britain 2001
This edition published 2003
by Egmont Books Limited
239 Kensington High Street, London W8 6SA
Missile Alert originally published as *Armed and Dangerous*
by Panini Comics, a division of Panini UK Ltd.

Licensed by:

Hasbro

Consumer
Products

ISBN 1 4052 0768 X

1 3 5 7 9 10 8 6 4 2

Printed and bound in China

ACTION MAN

MISSILE ALERT

EGMONT

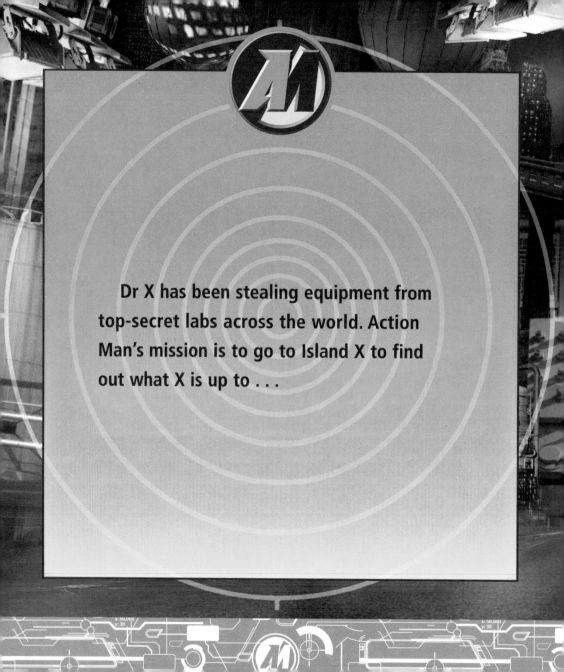

Dr X has been stealing equipment from top-secret labs across the world. Action Man's mission is to go to Island X to find out what X is up to . . .

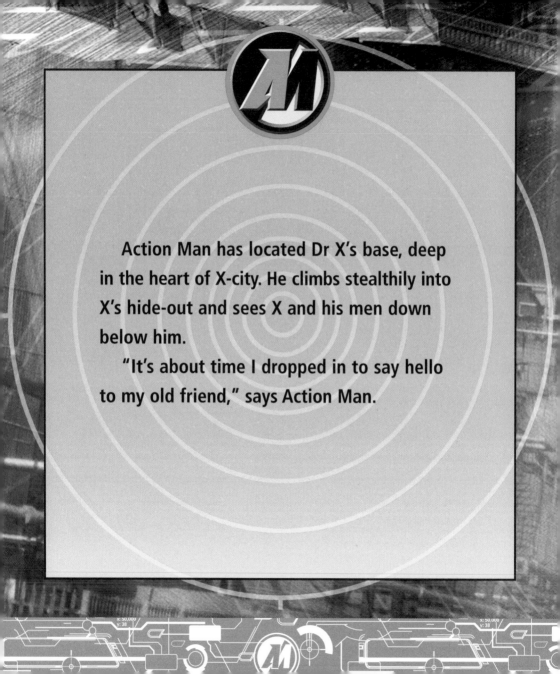

Action Man has located Dr X's base, deep in the heart of X-city. He climbs stealthily into X's hide-out and sees X and his men down below him.

"It's about time I dropped in to say hello to my old friend," says Action Man.

Dr X is about to launch the missiles he has stolen from around the world.

"My missiles are aimed at all the major world capitals," shouts X. "They'll soon know who's in charge. I'll be the new World Leader in no time. Ha ha!"

"Not so fast, X!" says Action Man, as he swings down from the roof and hurls an Action Boomerang at his old enemy.

"You're no match for me," laughs Dr X. He catches the boomerang and crushes it.

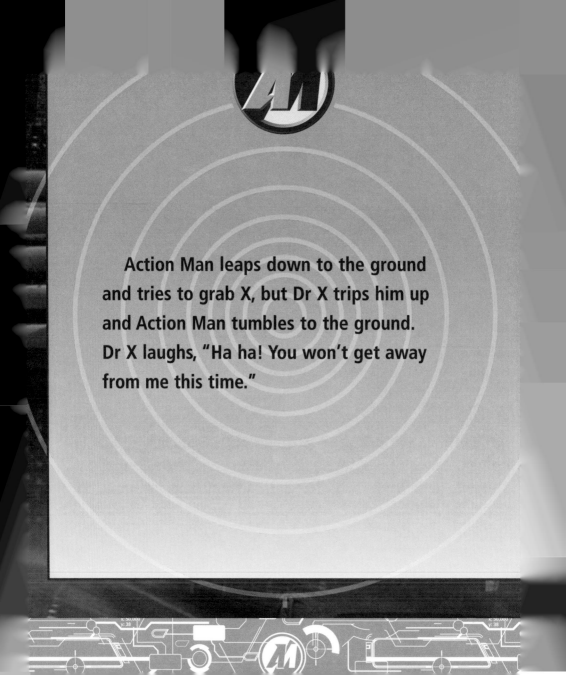

Action Man leaps down to the ground and tries to grab X, but Dr X trips him up and Action Man tumbles to the ground. Dr X laughs, "Ha ha! You won't get away from me this time."

"That's what you think!" says Action Man. He grabs another boomerang and throws it into the air. The next moment it returns and smashes into Dr X.

"What goes around, comes around!" says Action Man.

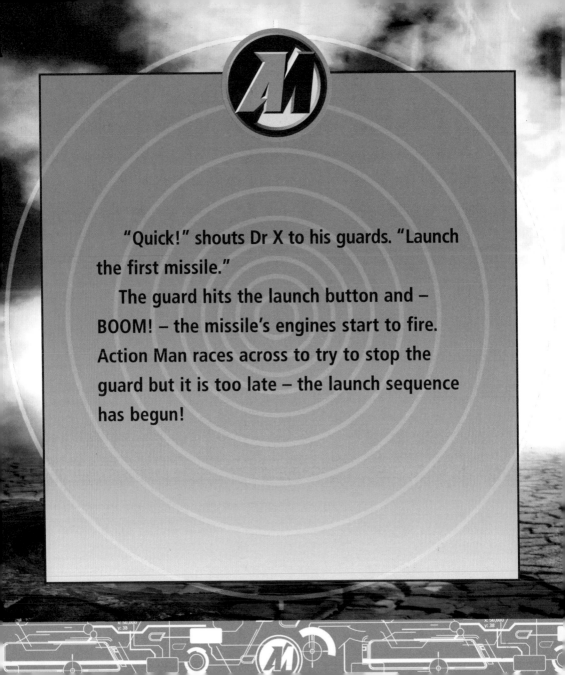

"Quick!" shouts Dr X to his guards. "Launch the first missile."

The guard hits the launch button and – BOOM! – the missile's engines start to fire. Action Man races across to try to stop the guard but it is too late – the launch sequence has begun!

"There's nothing you can do to stop me this time, Action Man," snarls Dr X. "Especially with only one boomerang left!"

But Action Man launches his boomerang again towards the guard and the next moment . . .

. . . he hits the computer controlling the missile's guidance system!

The missile turns around in midair and heads back on a collision course for X's base.

"Oh no," shouts Dr X. "My beautiful machines will be destroyed! You'll pay for this, Action Man!"

But Action Man has already scaled up his rope and out of X's base.

"Bye for now," Action Man says, "it's been a blast!"